TASHI
and the TIBETAN
FLOWER CURE

by NAOMI C. ROSE

Lee & Low Books Inc. *New York*

ACKNOWLEDGMENTS

Special thanks to Chime Dolker and her family, Tenzin Loden, Gyatso Dakchang, Debra Denkar, Renée Locks, Benjamin Long, Al Lustbader, Margaret Nevinski, Lee Paton, Robin Weeks, Christy Hale, and Louise May.

This book was inspired by the story "Downwind from Flowers" by Lee Paton, which also appeared in *Chicken Soup for the Gardener's Soul* by Jack Canfield, et al. I thank Ms. Paton for her generous spirit in allowing me to draw upon her true story.

LEE & LOW BOOKS Inc., 95 Madison Avenue, New York, NY 10016
leeandlow.com
Manufactured in Singapore by Tien Wah Press, June 2011
Book design by Christy Hale
Book production by The Kids at Our House
The text is set in Rotis Serif
The illustrations are rendered in acrylic on canvas
10 9 8 7 6 5 4 3 2 1
First Edition

Library of Congress Cataloging-in-Publication Data
Rose, Naomi C.
  Tashi and the Tibetan flower cure / by Naomi C. Rose. — 1st ed.
      p. cm.
  Includes notes about Tibet and Tibetan medicine as well as a glossary.
  Summary: "A young Tibetan American girl helps her grandfather recover from an illness through the use of a traditional cure that focuses on spiritual as well as physical recovery and brings together a caring community"—Provided by publisher.
  ISBN 978-1-60060-425-6 (hardcover : alk. paper)
[1. Grandfathers—Fiction. 2. Sick—Fiction. 3. Community life—Fiction. 4. Flowers—Fiction. 5. Tibetan Americans—Fiction.] I. Title.
  PZ7.R71782Tas 2011   [E]—dc22   2011010556

I love being with Popola
while he sings Tibetan chants.
My grandpa's deep voice
flows up and down
to the *click, click* of his *mala.*
I click my prayer beads too,
and the smoky smell of incense
fills the air.

For two weeks now
Popola has been in bed
making scratchy noises
with each breath.
I find Amala in the kitchen
and wrap my arms around her waist.
"When will Popola get better?" I ask.
Worry lines crowd my mama's face.
"I don't know, Tashi," she says.
"The doctor's doing
all she can."

Pots rattle on the stove,
spitting puffs of steam.
Amala smooths my bangs.
"Come," she says. "Time to eat."
She's made chicken and noodles—
my favorite.
But I'm not hungry.

Later I go to Popola's room
and arrange his pillows
so he can sit up better.
Candlelight flickers around the room
to where the *thangka* hangs.
Flowers glow on the painted scroll,
and I trace a petal with my eyes.
Flowers!
"Popola," I say. "Remember you told me
that sick people in your village
use flowers to get better?
How does it work?"
"Pollen from flowers
can help heal," he says.
"So we sit downwind
and let ourselves be dusted by pollen
that floats on the breeze."
Popola makes a slight, wavy movement
with his hand.
His eyes look far away.
I think he misses Tibet
and the people from his village.

I tell my best friend, Ben,
about the flower cure.
His mom lets us pick spring daisies
from their yard.

Back at home
Popola naps on the couch.
Ben holds the daisies
while I blow and blow.
Popola's nose twitches,
but he doesn't wake up.

The next day
Popola coughs a lot.
I tell Amala about the daisies:
how I blew and blew,
but the flower cure didn't work.
Amala holds me close.
"How sweet of you to try," she says.
"But you need lots of flowers."
"Oh," I say,
and rest my head on Amala's shoulder.

Ben and I ride our bikes
after school.
The air whooshes over me
as we glide along.
A sign says FLOWERS.
"Ben," I cry. "A flower nursery.
That's what Popola needs."
We zoom home and tell Amala.
"That could work," she says.

Sunday afternoon Amala and I
walk to the nursery,
where a man is watering plants
with purple buds.
"Hello," he says. "May I help you?"
Amala explains about Popola
and the flower cure.
"We need LOTS of flowers,"
I blurt out, then bite my lip,
wondering if he will help.
The man scratches his head.
"Never heard of that before," he says.
But then he puts down his watering can
and shakes our hands.
"I'm Sam Wong.
I would be happy to have you visit.
Why don't you come next Saturday?"
Amala and I swing our arms together
all the way home.

Popola joins us for dinner
but only eats a few bites of rice.
I tell him about the nursery.
"Can we try the flower cure?" I ask.
Popola shakes his head.
"No, no, no," he says.
"Why not?" I ask.
"Won't work here," he says,
"without the magic of our land
and people."
His face melts into a lonely gaze.
I blink back tears.
I feel lonely too,
with Popola sick.

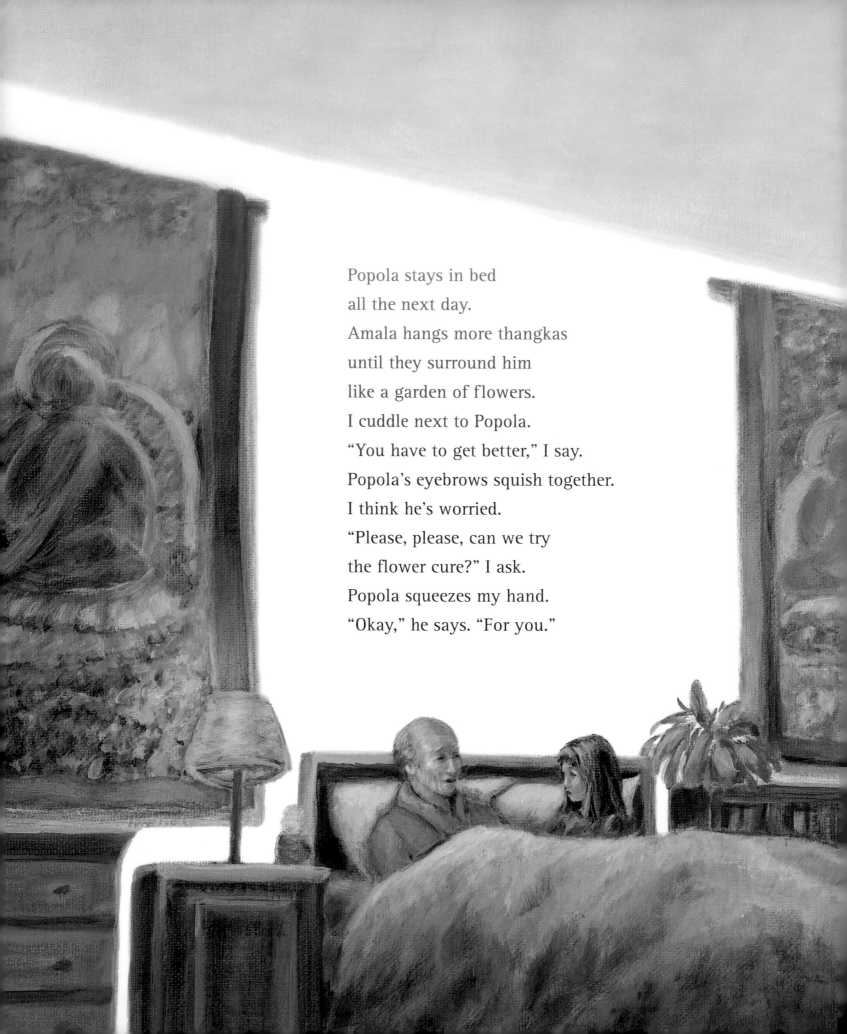

Popola stays in bed
all the next day.
Amala hangs more thangkas
until they surround him
like a garden of flowers.
I cuddle next to Popola.
"You have to get better," I say.
Popola's eyebrows squish together.
I think he's worried.
"Please, please, can we try
the flower cure?" I ask.
Popola squeezes my hand.
"Okay," he says. "For you."

I wake early on Saturday
and help Amala pack a basket
of black tea, butter, and salt,
cups and cookies,
and a thermos of hot water.
Once Popola is dressed,
we help him shuffle
into the car.

At the nursery
I catch a whiff of something sweet.
"Lilacs," says Mr. Wong.
He sets up folding chairs,
and Popola lowers himself into one
with a long sigh.
Amala brews the tea.
I add the butter and salt.
Then we pour the *solja* into cups.

We sip our tea
and eat our cookies.
Shoppers pass by but don't say hello.
"Is this what the flower cure is like
in Tibet?" I ask Popola.
"Many villagers sit together," he says.
He slumps in his chair
like a wilted leaf.
I slump too. Maybe he's right.
The flower cure won't work here.

Later Mr. Wong stops by.
"What else can I do to help?" he asks.
"Please sit down," says Popola.
"Drink our tea and eat our cookies."
Mr. Wong is nice.
He sits with us
and talks about flowers.
"Why don't you come again
next Saturday?" he asks.

Wind socks hang at the nursery
on our next visit.
Their striped colors flutter and dance,
and point downwind.
"We hung these for you,"
says Mr. Wong's assistant.
She leads us to chairs
near orange blossoms.
I remember Popola's words to Mr. Wong.
"Please sit down," I say.
"Drink our tea and eat our cookies."

She sits with us
and welcomes shoppers.
Amala serves them solja.
One of the shoppers is Ben's mom.
Ben's with her too.
We play while people talk in happy tones.
Popola sits up a little straighter.
But every time he coughs
my stomach twists.

On the following Saturday
Mr. Wong gives us different chairs.
"These should be more comfortable," he says.
He's right.
We sink into the soft cushions.
Amala pours solja
for all the shoppers
who come to greet Popola.
A man with a little dog
brings Popola a pot of roses.
I touch my nose
to the velvety petals.
"They smell like honey," I say.
Popola chuckles.
"You've got pollen
all over your nose," he says.
I haven't heard Popola laugh
since he got sick.

Sunflowers at the nursery grow
all summer long
until they're taller than me.
The days are hot,
but Mr. Wong sets up big umbrellas
to keep us cool.
Ben comes with us a lot.
We hand out cookies and tea
to all the people who visit Popola.
They have heard about the flower cure
and want to help.
"Here are some lilies. They're my favorite."
"I brought hot water to freshen the tea."
"Here's a pillow for your chair."
Popola's cheeks begin to glow
as pink as the potted poppies.

One Saturday Amala drives Popola
to the doctor.
My fingers fiddle
with a loose button on my shirt
while I wait.

Finally the car pulls into the driveway.
My heart races a hundred times faster
than my legs
as I run toward them.
"The doctor says I'm getting better,"
says Popola.
"Yay!" I shout.

The doorbell chimes
a short while later.
Amala opens the door.
Lots of people are there
with armfuls of flowers!
"We missed seeing you today
at Mr. Wong's nursery,"
says the man with the little dog.
"So we brought the flowers here."

Popola's face crinkles
into a big smile
as people stream into our backyard.
"All the flowers," says Popola.
"All the caring friends."
"Sort of like Tibet?" I ask.
Popola nods and hugs me close.
"Thank you, Tashi," he says.

In the backyard
Popola sings Tibetan chants.
His deep voice flows
up and down
to the *click, click* of his mala.
He sits tall,
all sunny and bright.
Pollen swirls, and my nose twitches.
"AHHH-CHOOO!"
Everyone laughs—
Popola and me
loudest of all.

TIBET

Tibet lies in central Asia among the Himalaya, the tallest mountain range in the world. The country's history is rich in mystical teachings, and its people are known for their kind and peaceful ways. Since 1959 the Chinese government has controlled Tibet. In search of spiritual and cultural freedom, hundreds of thousands of Tibetans have left their homeland to begin new lives in other countries, including the United States.

TIBETAN AMERICANS

Tibetans who immigrate to the United States settle in communities all around the country. They may live in areas with many other Tibetans or none at all. Like many immigrants, they face the challenges of preserving their culture, customs, and beliefs while adapting to American life. Tibetan Americans have set up cultural centers to help maintain their traditions. These centers also offer others in the community a chance to enjoy Tibetan culture through musical performances, ceremonies, and celebrations.

TIBETAN MEDICINE

Tibetans believe that many things have the power to heal the body, mind, and heart. A kind word or gesture, loving friends, cherished animals, nature, and music can all contribute to healing. Tibetans also use spiritual practices such as prayer and chanting to overcome illness, as well as other forms of suffering. When medicine is necessary, Tibetans prefer remedies created from substances found in nature, including herbs, trees, rocks, soils, precious metals, saps, pollens, and flowers.

TIBETAN WORDS

Amala* (AHM-ah-lah): Mama, Mom
mala (MAH-lah): string of Tibetan prayer beads
Popola* (POH-poh-lah): Grandpa
solja (SOHL-jah): Tibetan tea; made with black tea, butter, and salt
Tashi (TAH-she): Tibetan name for a male or female
thangka (TAHNG-kah): Tibetan scroll painting of sacred images and stories

*the "la" ending indicates respect and affection